Brad, the Fraidy Bat

by Liza Charlesworth
illustrated by Joseph Wilkins

ISBN: 979-8-225-02084-2

Publisher: Tara Welty
Creative Director: Tannaz Fassihi; Designer: Cynthia Ng

1 2 3 4 5 6 7 8 9 10 68 34 33 32 31 30 29 28 27 26 25

Made in Jiaxing City, China. First printing, August 2025.

SCHOLASTIC

Meet a brown bat named Brad.
He had long fangs and sharp claws.
He also had a pair of floppy wings
to flap across the dark night sky.
Was Brad brave? Nope, not a bit.

You see, Brad was just a big, fraidy bat who was scared to meet other creatures. For that reason, he had just one pal—a wise old owl named Oscar.

One October night, Oscar said to Brad, "Hoot, hoot! The moon is bright. Why don't you go out and try to make a few new pals?" Brad knew that Oscar was quite wise, so he waved his wing and said, "OK. Bye." He flapped up, up, up to a tall tower.

He flapped down, down, down to a garden.
What did he see? A blue spider making a web!
Spin, spin! The web looked just like lace.
Brad really wanted to say, "Nice work!"
But he had never met a spider before, so—
Flap, flap! That fraidy bat flew away.

Brad flapped and flapped and flapped.
Then he spotted a sleek black kitty
standing on top of a wide stone wall.
The kitty had soft fur and whiskers.
She had white paws and a long tail.

The kitty swished her tail as she gazed
up at the twinkling stars and purred.
Brad wished he had the guts to say,
"The sound you make is like music!"
But he hadn't met a kitty before, so—
Flap, flap! That fraidy bat flew away.

Brad flew until he spotted a rocky cave. There were lots of glowing lights inside it. What were they? Brad needed to know, so he hid behind a patch of tall grass. He waited and waited and then. . .

out of the cave stepped a mom raccoon,
plus one, two, three, four, five cute babies.
Golly, gee! The whole family was amazing.
But Brad hadn't met raccoons before, so—
Flap, flap! That fraidy bat flew away.

Brad flew high, low, and all around.
He flapped up, up, up to the top of a hill.
He flapped down, down, down to a pond.
Oh, my! The pond was as smooth as glass.
Brad stared into it, and what did he see?
He saw stars and the round white moon.
He also saw a fantastic creature.

Oh, my! The creature had brown fur.
He had long fangs and sharp claws.
He also had a pair of floppy wings.
One part of Brad wanted to meet him,
but the other part of Brad was afraid—
very, very, very afraid.

“Oh, why can’t I be brave!” cried Brad.
Then a really odd thing happened.
The pond creature cried just like him!
What in the world was going on?
Brad was just about to fly away. . .

when his pal Oscar landed in the tree beside him and said, "Hoot, hoot! Do NOT flap away in fear. You know the creature in the pond quite well. Who is he? He is YOU!"

“Yikes, Oscar! You are right!” Brad exclaimed. “The creature in the pond is my reflection, which means I was just afraid of. . .myself.” What did Brad do after that? He began to giggle and giggle. And when he giggled, the creature in the pond giggled, too.

At last, the giggles stopped and Oscar asked Brad this question: “Did you learn a lesson?”
“Yes,” replied Brad with a smile. “I learned that it is not good for me to be a fraidy bat. All of the creatures in the land are fantastic. I just need to be brave and go meet them!”
“You got it!” said Oscar. “My work is complete.”

What did the NOT-fraidy bat do after that?
He flew around and met the fine blue spider
and sleek black kitty and whole raccoon family.
Yippee! Brad could not decide which new pal
he liked best. . .so he hung out with all of them!